Ten Best Jewish Children's Stories

Retold by Chana and Daniel Sperber

Illustrated by Jeffrey Allon

PITSPOPANY

NEW YORK ◇ JERUSALEM

Published by PITSPOPANY PRESS
First cloth revised edition © 2000
Text Copyright © 1995 by Chana and Daniel Sperber
Illustrations Copyright © 1995 by Jeffrey Allon

PRINTING HISTORY
First Impression, November 1995
Second Impression, June 1996
Third Impression, June 2000

Pitspopany Press books may be purchased for educational
or special sales by contacting: Marketing Director,
Pitspopany Press, 40 East 78th Street, Suite 16D, New York, N. Y. 10021.
Fax: (212) 472-6253. E-mail: pop@netvision.net.il
Visit our website at: www.pitspopany.com

Design: Benjie Herskowitz

ISBN: 0-943706-58-0 Cloth
ISBN: 0-943706-86-6 Softcover

Printed in Hong Kong

With deepest gratitude and appreciation
to our beloved parents
Nana and Papa

C.S./D.S.

For Shelly, Ariel, Liana, Ashira,
Neveh and Ma'ayan.
And for my parents, Michael and Marcella Allon

J.A.

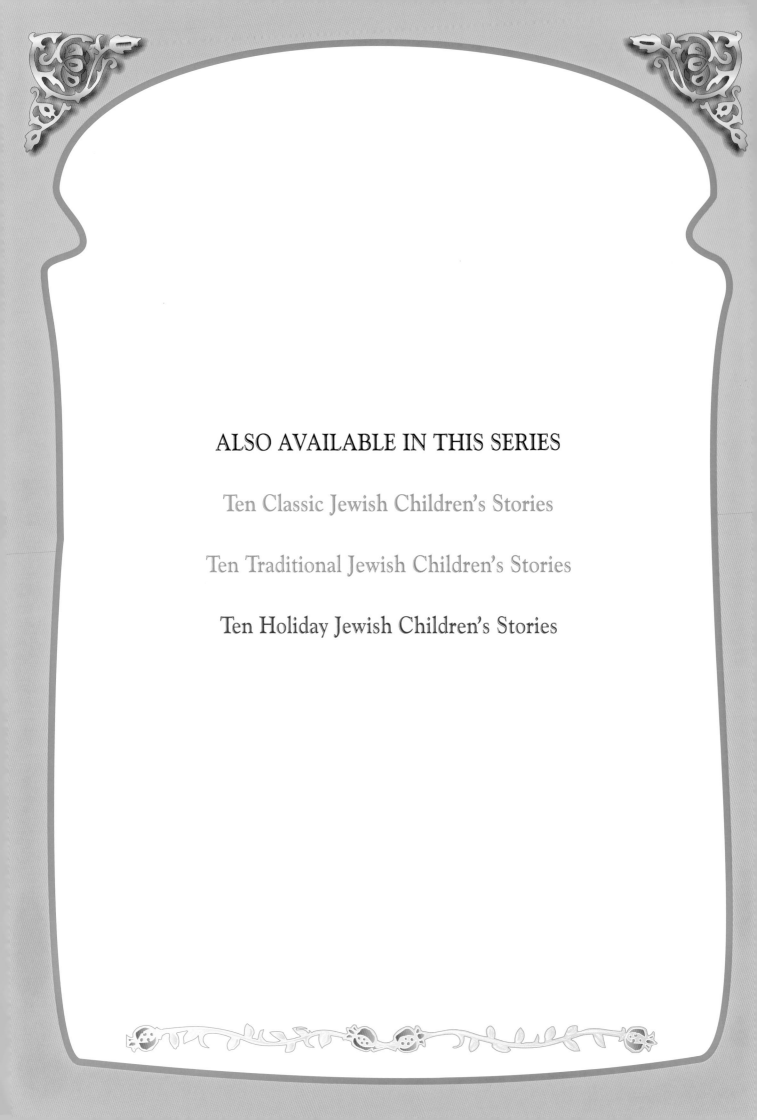

ALSO AVAILABLE IN THIS SERIES

Ten Classic Jewish Children's Stories

Ten Traditional Jewish Children's Stories

Ten Holiday Jewish Children's Stories

Table of Contents

Jewish Storytelling
by Peninnah Schram

IT WAS THE ROLE OF THE STORYTELLER in the Jewish oral tradition to keep Jewish laws, values, traditions and customs alive for centuries, including the ages of persecution and isolation that Jewish communities had to endure. Parents and grandparents, who understood this role as essential, were part of a chain that shared the Biblical and Rabbinical commandments from one generation to another. But the commandments were just the tip of the legacy. What families were ultimately trying to transmit to the children through these stories was an almost indefinable concept – a feeling for Jewish tradition, a pathway to God which would create in their children what the Jewish world calls *menschlichkeit.*

Menschlichkeit – the state of being a compassionate empathetic person who performs good deeds – is a trait that could be taught, not only by studying the Torah, the Prophets, and the Talmud, but by the quintessential teaching tool, the *mah-seh*, the story, the parable. These Rabbinic tales showed that evil existed, and was strong, but also that good existed, and could be even stronger.

Whether leisurely plucking goose feathers, or preparing for Shabbat, Jewish mothers constantly told stories that would help their children become *menschen.* The idea was to entertain and yet, at the same time, challenge the child through an imaginative story. In this way, children could discover for themselves the important Jewish value, commandment, or Rabbinical law they needed to integrate into their own lives.

What kind of stories are the "best" stories?

Many of the best stories deal with fascinating questions of relationships and ethics, in a non-threatening way, such as, "Why is there injustice in the world?" and "Why do bad things happen to good people?" In order to teach these lessons, the main characters of the stories are often poor, humble people. Being poor, while not a virtue, was not something to be ashamed of. After all, people always had the possibility of bettering themselves. Of course, while the character may be poor in material wealth, he is usually rich in faith and performance of good deeds which are the greatest treasures. As an illustration of this, let's look at two of the stories in this book.

In IT'S ALL FOR THE BEST, young Rabbi Akiva, poor and out of work, is beset with one tragedy after another, and yet he never ceases to praise God: "Everything God does is for the best," he exclaims after each hair-raising experience. While a child may wonder at the ability of Rabbi Akiva to look disaster in the eye and smile, the child soon learns that sometimes personal disaster can be a blessing, if God wills it.

GOD'S HIDDEN WAYS deals with this same theme, but from a skeptic's approach. The wise Rabbi Yehoshua ben Levi knows everything except "Why do good people sometimes suffer, while wicked ones prosper?" His belief cannot be whole until he has an answer. The answer comes from the folktale hero, Elijah the Prophet. The Rabbi is permitted a glance behind the veil that surrounds the doubter, and his faith is fully restored.

Both these stories are keys to the development of menschlichkeit. They present insights into the meaning of the commandments, but most importantly, they serve as a vehicle for children to ask their own questions about God, without fear, without hesitation.

Other stories, like MORE VALUABLE THAN GOLD, teach that menschlichkeit is not a specifically Jewish phenomenon, but a desirable human trait. In this ancient tale, a gentile, Dama, has the opportunity to make a fortune if he will only unlock the box that holds a unique precious gem. But the key to the box is under his father's pillow. Dama refuses to wake up his father, not for all the gold in the world. From this tale, the child creatively understands, not only about the importance of honoring one's parents, but also about the need to learn from all people how to behave.

Each of these stories is included in this book because it is one of the best stories that has been lovingly retold from parent to child. The telling of these stories creates a common core of tradition and values which can be passed on to new generations.

How Could It Be Worse?

Traditional Jewish Folktale

Miriam and Samuel lived with their seven children in a one-room house. Next to the house there was a little barn where they kept a cow, a donkey, and a goat. Miriam and Samuel loved their children dearly, but felt they were a bit too noisy.

Esther played the flute: "tweet, tweet, tweet!" Elisheva sang: "tra-la-la-la-lee!" Abigail jumped rope: "swoosh, swoosh, swoosh!" Sarah tossed her jacks on the floor: "clack, clack, clack!" Yehuda bounced his ball hard: "boom, boom, boom!" And David and Joseph learned Talmud all day in the traditional sing-song tune, chanting in Aramaic: "tanya nami hachi."

One day Samuel turned to his wife and asked, "What shall we do? This constant noise is driving me insane! I can't think during the day and I can't sleep during the night!"

"Let's speak to the Rabbi," suggested Miriam. "Perhaps he'll have an answer."

That evening, Samuel and Miriam knocked on the Rabbi's door. "Please come in," said the Rabbi. "Have some tea and tell me your problem."

"Our home is too noisy, by far," Samuel complained.

"Our children are very good," added Miriam, "but the noise is a problem. And with nine of us in one room, we're feeling terribly crowded!"

The Rabbi thought for a moment. Then he announced, "I know just the thing that you should do. Bring your cow into the house."

"What! Are you sure?" Gasped Samuel.

"Quite sure," said the Rabbi.

So Miriam and Samuel brought the cow into the house.

"MOO," said the cow. Esther tweeted. Elisheva tra-la-la-laed. Abigail swooshed. Sarah clacked. Yehuda boomed. David and Joseph chanted "tanya nami hachi."

"What an awful clatter!" groaned Miriam and Samuel.

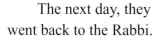

The next day, they went back to the Rabbi. "Rabbi, Rabbi," they cried as he opened the door, "the noise is worse than before!"

"Trust me," said the Rabbi. "Now bring your donkey into the house.

Although this advice sounded strange, they did as the Rabbi commanded.

"HEE-HAW-HEE-HAW," brayed the donkey. "MOO" said the cow. Esther tweeted. Elisheva tra-la-laed. Abigail swooshed. Sarah clacked. Yehuda boomed. David and Joseph chanted "tanya nami hachi." And Miriam and Samuel thought they would go crazy!

So, back to the Rabbi they went.

"Things are proceeding according to plan," he told them. "Now bring your goat into the house."

"What good will that do?" they wondered. But they certainly weren't going to interfere with the Rabbi's plan. So, they brought in the goat.

In the middle of the night, after everyone was already asleep, the goat bleated "BAA-BAA-BAA" and ate Yehuda's blanket.

The whole family woke up. Soon there was tweeting and tra-la-la-laing and swooshing and clacking and booming and chanting and mooing and braying.

"Let's go back to the Rabbi," moaned Miriam. "We can't possibly go on like this!"

And so, back to the Rabbi they went.

"Dear Rabbi," they cried as they rushed in. "Forgive us for disturbing you so late at night, but you must help us."

"Don't worry," he assured them. "Now, take the cow, and the donkey, and the goat back into the barn."

They rushed home and did as the Rabbi said.

That next day Esther tweeted. Elisheva tra-la-la-laed. Abigail swooshed. Sarah clacked. Yehuda boomed. David and Joseph chanted "tanya nami hachi." But Miriam just gazed lovingly at her family.

"Samuel," she sighed, "how lucky we are! We have food to eat, a roof over our heads, good health, and best of all, seven wonderful children who barely utter a sound!"

NOW CONSIDER THIS:

❋ *Why is this story called "How Could It Be Worse?"*

❋ *What was the Rabbi's plan?*

❋ *What did Miriam and Samuel learn from the Rabbi's advice?*

❋ *What questions would you like to ask a Rabbi?*

For The Love Of Two Brothers

Traditional Jewish Legend

In the days before the Temple was built, two brothers, Shimon and Levi, inherited a large field from their parents. The field was on Mount Moriah in the heart of the Land of Israel.

"Should we work the field together?" Shimon, the oldest brother asked, "Or divide it into two separate fields?"

"I'd like to share it with you, Shimon," Levi replied. "What do you think?"

"That sounds good to me," the older brother answered.

So they worked together year after year. At harvest time, they cut the wheat, bound it into sheaves, counted the number of sheaves and divided them equally into two piles.

Then each brother carried his pile to his own storehouse.

One year after harvesting all day in the sun, Shimon turned to Levi and said, "I'm too tired to take my wheat home. I will sleep here in the field beside my stacks."

"That's a good idea," said Levi. "I'm also exhausted. I'll sleep near my sheaves at the other side of the field."

But Shimon could not fall asleep. He kept thinking, "It isn't fair that my brother and I divide the harvest equally. He has a family to support and I am alone. Why should I take so much?"

So, at midnight Shimon got up and gathered as many sheaves as he could carry. He placed them on his brother's stack and quickly returned to his own side of the field. "I feel happy now," he murmured as he fell asleep.

Just after midnight, Levi awoke. He had dreamed about his brother.

In his dream he saw Shimon old and sick. "My poor brother," he thought to himself. "He is all alone. It's not right that we divide the grain equally between us. He has no wife or children. Who will help him when he is old? He must have more grain so he can prepare for that time."

Levi got up and carried as many sheaves as he could across the field to his brother's pile. Then he went back to his own stack and fell peacefully asleep.

In the morning, each brother loaded his sheaves onto his own wagon. Each was amazed to find that he had exactly the same number as before.

"This is very strange," thought Levi. "Did I only dream that I carried sheaves to my brother's pile last night?"

"How can this be?" Shimon wondered, as he looked at his sheaves piled high.

All that day the brothers worked, carrying the sheaves into their storehouses. When night came, they were very tired, but neither of them could sleep. They waited until midnight. Then each went to his storehouse and took as many sheaves as he could carry and walked quickly in the direction of his brother's house.

Shimon thought, "I want my brother's wife and children to have enough to eat."

And Levi thought, "Shimon must have a larger share of the harvest to help him in the years to come."

Suddenly, halfway between their homes, the two brothers saw each other in the moonlit field.

Shimon called out, "Levi, is that you? Now I understand what happened to my sheaves!"

Levi replied, "And now I understand what happened with *my* sheaves! You always think more about me and my family than about yourself!"

The two brothers rushed joyfully towards each other. With hearts full of love, they hugged each other tightly.

And it was that very spot, on top of Mount Moriah, that God chose for the site of the Holy Temple. And the Temple was filled with the same love and kindness that filled the hearts of those two brothers.

NOW CONSIDER THIS:

❊ *Do you remember a time that you shared something with someone you loved?*

❊ *Do you think it was right that each brother got half the wheat, or should one have gotten more?*

❊ *Why do you think the Holy Temple was built on Mount Moriah?*

❊ *Do you know what happened in the Bible to Isaac on Mount Moriah?*

God's Hidden Ways

Hibbur Yafeh – Mei HaYishuah

Rabbi Yehoshua ben Levi was a wise scholar and a righteous man. People came from near and far to ask his advice. But there was one question even he could not answer: "Why do good people sometimes suffer, while wicked people often prosper?"

One day Rabbi Yehoshua saw an old man leaning on a cane. "Good day, sir," he greeted him. "Are you new to our city?"

"Yes," the man replied. "I am Eliyahu HaNavi (the prophet Elijah). God sent me to you."

Rabbi Yehoshua was overjoyed. "For years I have prayed for the wisdom to understand God's hidden ways. Please tell me, why do good people sometimes suffer while wicked people often prosper?"

"Come with me," replied Eliyahu, "and see how I carry out God's plan on earth. This may help you to understand."

They walked together all day long. Towards evening a rainstorm broke out. They were both tired and soaked to the skin.

Just then, a man and a woman came out of a hut and ran in the pouring rain to a thin cow tied up in their yard.

"Come out of the rain, you poor old girl," said the woman to the cow. "I'll soon have you dried off and in your shed."

The couple saw Rabbi Yehoshua and Eliyahu watching them.

"Please gentlemen," the man said, "come into our home. You can sleep in our house tonight."

So Eliyahu and Rabbi Yehoshua entered the couple's hut. The man seated them on the only chairs in the house, while his wife served hot milk and bread.

"Please forgive me for not offering you more," she said, "but this is all we have."

Later, before he fell asleep, Rabbi Yehoshua heard Eliyahu pray for the couple's cow to die. "How could this be?" he wondered. "Perhaps I didn't hear right!"

16

But in the morning, he heard the woman cry out to her husband, "Our poor cow is dead, struck by lightning just as I sat down to milk her!"

Rabbi Yehoshua's heart was filled with anger and sorrow. "Is this the reward these kind and generous people deserve?" he asked himself.

As if reading his mind, Eliyahu raised his finger and warned, "If you question my actions, I will leave and you will learn nothing."

Eliyahu and Rabbi Yehoshua set out again. Towards evening, they reached the home of a very rich man. They knocked on the door. The man called out, "Who is it?"

"We are tired and hungry travelers," Eliyahu replied. "Please let us have something to eat and a place to sleep."

"There's no food here for lazy beggars," the man said, not even opening the door. "I have my own troubles. The wall at the back of my house fell down and none of the workmen showed up to fix it. Sleep in the garden, if you must," he told them, "but be gone at dawn."

At dawn, Eliyahu and Rabbi Yehoshua got up. Their bodies ached from lying on the cold stone bench. Eliyahu began to pray for God to fix the broken wall in the wealthy man's house. Immediately the wall rose up and fixed itself!

Rabbi Yehoshua was furious. He turned to Eliyahu and cried out, "You pray for bad things to happen to good people and good things happen to the wicked. Why?"

"You have questioned my actions and so I must leave," said Eliyahu sternly. "But first I will explain what you have seen. Lightning was going to strike the poor man's wife when she went to milk the cow. I prayed to God that she might live and that the cow be struck instead."

"And as for the wealthy miser, underneath the broken wall lies hidden a treasure of gold. The miser will be overjoyed that his wall was miraculously repaired. What he doesn't know is that the miracle prevented him from finding the gold."

"Always remember," concluded Eliyahu, "the ways of God are hidden. Not everything is as it appears to be. Not everything that seems good is really good, and not everything that seems bad is really bad."

And then, just as suddenly as he had appeared, Eliyahu vanished!

NOW CONSIDER THIS:

✳ *Can you remember something you thought was bad that turned out to be good?*

✳ *Why do you think that good things sometimes happen to bad people?*

✳ *What do you know about miracles?*

It's All For The Best

Babylonian Talmud. Ta'anit 21A

When Rabbi Akiva was young, he was very poor. But, though his life was hard, he never complained. No matter what happened to him, he always said, "Everything God does is for the best."

Once, Akiva set out to find work. As was his custom, he took all his possessions along with him. He had a rooster that woke him so he could pray early in the morning, a lamp for light during the night, and a donkey to ride on and carry his clothes and food.

Akiva travelled from place to place asking for work, but everyone said, "Sorry, we have no need for anyone today." By evening, he was very tired and far from home. He rode into a village and knocked on the door of the first house he saw.

"I'm very tired, and far away from home," Akiva told the owner of the house. "Perhaps you could let me sleep in your barn for the night?"

"Sorry," said the villager curtly. "We have no room anywhere!"

Akiva went to the next house, but the same thing happened. He went from house to house, but no one in the whole village would let him in.

So, with his coat for a blanket and a rock for a pillow, Akiva decided he would have to sleep in a deserted field. But he wasn't upset. "It doesn't matter," he said to himself. "Everything that God does is for the best!"

Sitting in the field, Akiva tried to light his lamp. It took a long time, for in those days there were no matches. Akiva rubbed two flint stones together until they finally sparked and lit a dry twig. He then transferred the fire to the wick in the oil lamp.

"Good," he said. "Now I can feed my donkey and rooster, eat something myself, and go to sleep."

Just then, a gust of wind blew out the lamp. "It doesn't matter," said Akiva. "Everything that God does is for the best!"

Akiva tried to light the lamp again. Suddenly he heard a fierce "Gr-rowl!

Growl!" followed by a frightened, "Cockle-doodle-do!"

"What is this crowing in the middle of the night?" he wondered. When he went to look, an awful sight met his eyes. A panther had eaten up his rooster!

"How terrible!" he cried. "Poor thing. But everything God does is for the best!"

Just then Akiva heard another noise, "Hee-haw, hee-haw. Ee-yai! Ee-yai!"

"Now, what could be the matter with my donkey?" he asked himself. As Akiva ran to have a look, he heard an ear-splitting "RO-O-O-AR!" An enormous lion had made a tasty supper of Akiva's beast!

"How awful!" he thought.

Now Akiva had no light, no rooster, and no donkey. But what do you think he said? That's right. He said, "Everything that God does is for the best!"

A few hours later Akiva heard loud voices. He saw a group of men nearby with swords and daggers that shone in the moonlight! They were drunken pirates who had come up from the coast to attack the nearby village. Akiva kept very still. The men passed by without noticing him.

"How fortunate that I had no light or they would certainly have seen me," Akiva thought gratefully. "And if they had heard my animals, they might have killed me. Everything that God does is for the best."

But the nearby village was not so lucky. The pirates captured the villagers and emptied their houses of everything valuable. Then they burned the village down. In the morning, when Akiva passed through, there was nothing left at all!

"If I had been given a place to sleep here last night," he thought, "I, too, would have been carried away! Everything that God does is truly for the best!"

Later, Akiva worked as a shepherd for a wealthy landowner. He married the man's daughter, Rachel, and with her help became the famous scholar, Rabbi Akiva.

NOW CONSIDER THIS:

✳ *What does "Everything that God does is for the best!" mean to you?*

✳ *What is a scholar? Do you know any scholars?*

✳ *Why do you think the villagers were punished?*

Nicanor's Doors

Jerusalem Talmud. Yoma 3:10;
Babylonian Talmud. Yoma 38A

Once there was a wealthy Jew named Nicanor, who lived in the city of Alexandria in Egypt. Three times a year, on Succot, Passover, and Shavuot, Nicanor travelled to Jerusalem to pray in the Holy Temple.

Whenever he entered the Temple Mount, Nicanor said to himself, "Here in this place I can feel God's loving Spirit watching over me. I want to give a gift to the Temple to show my love for God and the Jewish people. But what should I give?"

He thought and thought. "I will hire the best craftsmen in Egypt to make beautiful bronze doors for the Temple courtyard," Nicanor decided.

For a whole year Nicanor searched for the best bronze in Egypt. It was as strong as iron and as shiny as gold. It took two years for the workers to make the doors, for Nicanor insisted they had to be perfect.

"Why do you spend so much time and money on these doors?" the people asked Nicanor.

"With God's help, these doors will stand in the holiest place on earth," replied Nicanor. "They must be perfect!"

At last the doors were ready. They were truly splendid. Nicanor could hardly wait to see them standing in the House of God. He hired fifty strong porters to carry them to the dock and load them onto a ship sailing to the Land of Israel. Nicanor went along, too.

While at sea, a fierce storm broke out. The boat rocked back and forth. Huge waves flooded the deck. The boat was going to sink!

"The boat is too heavy," cried the sailors. "We must throw something overboard, or else we will all drown!"

"Nicanor's doors are the biggest and heaviest items on board," said the captain. "We must throw them into the sea right now!" he commanded.

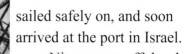

Nicanor's face went pale. His eyes filled with tears. "Please sir," he begged, "don't throw my beautiful doors into the sea. There must be another way to save the ship."

But the waves rose up even higher, and the sailors were very frightened. Without waiting another second, they threw one of the doors overboard. Nicanor looked on, heartbroken, as his precious door sank under the waves.

Then the sailors brought up the second door.

"No! Wait!" Nicanor yelled.

But the waves continued to toss the ship back and forth. The sailors lifted up the second door, preparing to throw it into the sea. Nicanor rushed over and hugged the door.

"If you throw this door into the sea," he shouted, "you will have to throw me in too!"

The sailors paused for a moment. What should they do?

Then something amazing happened! The storm suddenly stopped. The sea became as smooth as glass. The ship sailed safely on, and soon arrived at the port in Israel.

Nicanor got off the ship and watched as the porters carried the one remaining door down the ramp. He was glad that the boat hadn't sunk, but he was still sad that one of his beautiful doors had ended up at the bottom of the sea.

He tearfully looked out at the sparkling waves and heaved a sigh, when suddenly, up popped the other door and stood itself next to its twin!

Everyone was astonished. "How can this be?" they asked.

Nicanor was overjoyed. "My shining door is here!" he exclaimed, running over to touch it. "And it's still perfect! It's a miracle, a wondrous miracle!"

Soon his joy was complete. The splendid doors were installed at the eastern gate of the Holy Temple where they glistened like gold in the bright morning sunlight. And from that day on, the eastern gate was called the Gate of Nicanor, to honor the man who was so loyal and generous in his devotion to God and His people.

NOW CONSIDER THIS:

✳ Why did Nicanor want to give a present to the Temple?

✳ Do you think it was right for Nicanor to threaten to jump into the sea with his door?

✳ How is the story of Jonah and the whale similar to the story of Nicanor's doors? How is it different?

More Valuable Than Gold

Jerusalem Talmud. Pe'ah 1:1;
Babylonian Talmud. Kiddushin 31A

In the days when the Jewish people worshipped in their Holy Temple in Jerusalem, one special man led the High Holiday prayers. He was the High Priest and he wore a splendid garment decorated with twelve beautiful jewels. Each jewel represented one of the twelve tribes of Israel. These jewels lit up and spelled out secret messages from God.

One day someone noticed that the blue-green jasper stone was gone. He quickly ran to get the Rabbis.

"Look," he exclaimed, "the Tribe of Benjamin's jewel is missing!"

The Rabbis wasted no time. They took a large sum of gold coins from the Temple treasury and set out to buy a new stone. They went searching from city to city.

"Where can we buy a large and perfect blue-green jasper stone?" they asked. But no one knew, for such a stone is very hard to find.

After weeks of searching, the Rabbis met a jeweller who said, "In Caesarea, a gentile named Dama ben Netina has a collection of the most unusual jewels in the land of Israel. Maybe he can help you."

The Rabbis rushed off to find Dama. They knocked on his door, and he showed them in.

"We have come to buy a blue-green jasper stone," said the Rabbis. "If you have one, we will pay you one hundred gold coins for it."

"I have just the gem you want, and I will be happy to sell it to you," said Dama. "Please be seated while I bring the key to my jewel box."

The Rabbis were thankful to have found the gem at last.

Dama ran to his bedroom to get the key from under his pillow where he kept it hidden. But when he reached the bed he saw his father lying there, fast asleep.

"If I try to pull the key out from under the pillow, I might wake my father," he thought. "This I must not do."

Dama returned to the Rabbis and said, "I am sorry, but I cannot

sell you the jasper stone right now."

"He must want more money," the Rabbis whispered to each other. "After all, it is a very rare jewel." And so they offered two hundred gold coins for the gem.

But Dama replied, "No, I cannot sell it to you, even for two hundred gold coins."

The Rabbis offered him three hundred, then four hundred and finally five hundred gold coins.

But each time, Dama refused to sell them the jewel.

Now the Rabbis were desperate. "Kind sir," they pleaded, making their last offer, "sell us the jewel and we will pay you one thousand gold coins!"

But Dama wouldn't budge! "I cannot sell you the jasper stone for all the gold in the world," he insisted. So the Rabbis left, very disappointed.

An hour later, when his father woke up from his nap, Dama got the key and opened the box. He took out the gem and rushed out to find the Rabbis.

"Here is your gem," he announced, out of breath, when at last he caught up to them.

"And here are your one thousand gold coins," the Rabbis said, happily handing him the sacks of money.

"You only owe me the one hundred coins that you offered in the first place," Dama told them. "I did not sell you the stone earlier because I could not get the key without waking my father. Once he woke up it was a simple matter to get the jewel you asked for. One hundred gold coins is fine. I certainly don't want to profit for honoring my father as I should."

The Rabbis paid one hundred coins for the jasper stone and returned to Jerusalem. There at the Temple they told the people, "Let us all learn from Dama ben Netina how to fulfill the commandment of honoring one's father."

NOW CONSIDER THIS:

❋ *Honor Your Father and Mother is one of the Ten Commandments. What other commandments do you know?*

❋ *How do you honor your mother and father?*

❋ *Can you find the names of the twelve tribes of Israel and their special stones in the picture on the next page?*

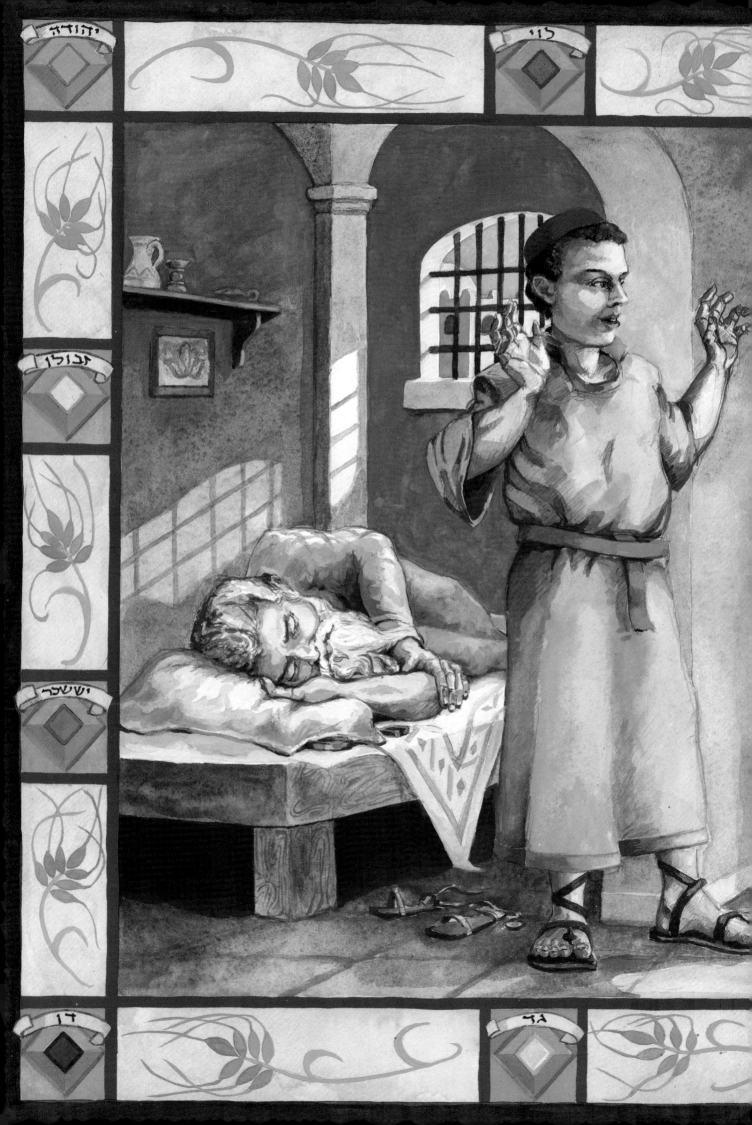

The Chickens That Turned Into Goats

Babylonian Talmud. Ta'anit 25A and Berachot 17B

Rabbi Hanina ben Dosa and his wife Naomi were very poor. On most days the family ate just dry vegetables and carobs from the tree in their yard.

One summer day, a man came to the village where Rabbi Hanina lived. He carried two large sacks filled with vegetables. He sold one sack at the marketplace and, with the money he received, he bought chickens. He put the chickens in a box and tied the box with a red string.

It was a very hot day, so the man looked for a cool place to rest. When he reached Rabbi Hanina's yard, he decided to rest under the shady carob tree. He put the sack and the box of chickens down beside him. Then he leaned back and fell asleep. When he awoke, the sun was setting.

"I must hurry to the marketplace," he said, "and sell the rest of my vegetables before it gets dark."

He quickly lifted the heavy sack and ran off, leaving the box of chickens under the carob tree.

"They're safe here," he thought. "I'll come back and get them later."

By the time the man went back to get his chickens it was already dark. He searched everywhere for the carob tree, but couldn't find it.

"How disappointed my family will be not to have those chickens!" he thought, as he set out for home.

Meanwhile, the chickens grew hungry and started making noise. "Cluck! Cluck! Cackle! Cackle!" they clucked and cackled.

Naomi went outside to see what was making all that ruckus. She found the chickens in the box that was tied with a red string. She looked everywhere but she couldn't find the owner.

Naomi took the chickens inside and asked her husband, "What shall we do with them?"

"Someone must have forgotten them here," replied Rabbi Hanina. "We'll take care of them until their owner returns."

Naomi fed the chickens and gave them water. Soon, the hens began to lay eggs. "Look," said Naomi, "Now we can have eggs at our Sabbath meal!"

"No," said Rabbi Hanina. "We may not eat the eggs. They don't belong to us. The owner will surely come back for them."

The hens sat on their eggs. The eggs hatched into little chicks. The chicks grew into more hens and roosters. More eggs. More chickens. Soon, the house and yard were filled with hens and roosters. But no one came to claim the chickens!

"We cannot go on like this," said Naomi to her husband. "We must get rid of these chickens or we will have nothing left to eat."

"Why don't we sell all the chickens and buy goats instead," suggested Rabbi Hanina. "The goats will go out to the hillside by themselves to eat and you will have less work."

So they traded the chickens for three goats.

A few years went by and now there were ten goats in the shed. One day the owner of the chickens walked past Rabbi Hanina's home. He saw the carob tree and thought to himself, "This looks like the spot where I left my box of chickens! I wonder what happened to them?"

The man knocked on Rabbi Hanina's door. "Did you find a box of chickens here several years ago?" he asked.

"Yes we did. Do you remember what color they were and what kind of string was around their box?" asked Rabbi Hanina.

"The chickens were brown and the box was tied with a red string," the man replied.

Rabbi Hanina smiled. "I have something to show you," he said, and led the man to the shed. "Here are your chickens."

The man looked around the shed. "I don't see any chickens here, only goats!"

Rabbi Hanina said, "Your chickens multiplied so quickly that my wife had to exchange them for goats. We have saved them for you and now they are all yours."

"Rabbi," said the man, "I have never heard of anyone looking after lost property like you and your wife have done! How can I thank you? Please, take one of the goats as a reward."

"No," said Rabbi Hanina ben Dosa, "we deserve no reward. We were only doing what the Torah commands. If you want to give thanks, then by all means, thank God."

NOW CONSIDER THIS:

✻ *Have you ever found a lost article? What did you do with it?*

✻ *Why did Rabbi Hanina ask the man to identify his chickens?*

The Scorpion And The Wedding

Babylonian Talmud. Shabbat 156B

Rabbi Akiva's daughter, Rivka, was the most beautiful woman in all the Land of Israel.

One day the Emperor's son, Prince Antoninus, saw Rivka at the town well and fell in love with her. He went to Rabbi Akiva and asked for her hand in marriage. Rabbi Akiva politely explained that his daughter could only marry a Jew. The prince promised Rabbi Akiva money and honor, but the Rabbi refused. Finally, the prince became very angry and shouted, "If I can't marry your daughter, then no one will. You will be sorry for this!"

A few days later the royal Roman sorcerer arrived at the House of Study where Rabbi Akiva spent most of his time learning. When the sorcerer saw the Rabbi, he threw some magic dust into the air and whispered, "On the very day that your daughter, Rivka, gets married, a scorpion will bite her and she will die."

Rabbi Akiva was upset about the sorcerer's evil spell, but he trusted in God and never spoke of it to anyone.

Some months later Rivka was engaged to be married. Everyone was happy, except Rabbi Akiva. He was worried about the sorcerer's curse. But he didn't say a word to Rivka. "It won't help to frighten her and spoil her happiness," he thought.

The wedding was a splendid affair. Many important people came. Everyone sang and danced. Then they all sat down to eat. Rivka was quite hungry for she had fasted before the wedding, as is the custom of brides and grooms to this very day.

When she got up to wash her hands before the meal, she heard a tapping at the door of the wedding hall. No one else heard it, because they were all too busy eating, drinking and talking. Rivka opened the door. There stood a man dressed in rags. He was very thin and his eyes were sad.

"Please sir," said Rivka. "Come in and eat something with us."

"Thank you kindly," the man replied, "but I cannot come in. My wife gave birth this afternoon to our sixth child. We have no money left and no

36

food in the house. Do you have something I can take to my family?"

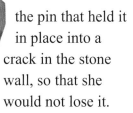

Rivka quickly filled two baskets with all the food she could find. Then she returned with the man to his home.

When they arrived, she heard the children crying, "Mommy, we are so hungry. Please give us something to eat!"

A weary, gentle voice answered, "Children, there is nothing to eat. Be patient. God will surely answer our prayers."

Rivka helped the poor man feed his children. She brought food and drink to the mother and helped make her and the baby comfortable. Then she hurried back to the wedding banquet.

By this time, the meal had ended and the guests were joyfully reciting the seven special blessings for the newlywed couple. Rivka still hadn't eaten, but she slipped quietly back to her place.

That night, before she went to sleep, Rivka took off her wedding veil. She put the pin that held it in place into a crack in the stone wall, so that she would not lose it.

In the morning when she took it out of the crack, she cried out, "Look! A dead creature is stuck on the end of my pin!"

"It's a scorpion!" exclaimed her husband. "Your pin pierced it right through the eye!"

When the newlyweds told Rabbi Akiva about the scorpion, he rushed to see for himself.

"What good deed did you perform that saved you from death?" he asked his daughter.

She told him about the beggar and how she had missed the feast on her wedding night. He thought to himself, "It was surely this act of charity and kindness that saved her from the sorcerer's curse. Even curses are rendered harmless when we do God's commandments with all our heart."

NOW CONSIDER THIS:

✤ *Why didn't Rabbi Akiva agree to the Roman prince's request to marry his daughter?*

✤ *What acts of charity have you done?*

✤ *Why do you think newlyweds fast on the day of their wedding?*

✤ *How is this story also an example of the famous saying, "Love your neighbor as yourself"?*

The Shadow On The House Of Study

Babylonian Talmud. Yoma 35B

There was once a man named Hillel who loved to learn Torah. He loved to learn so much that he left his family in Babylonia and went to Jerusalem to study with the great scholars, Shemaya and Avtalyon.

To support himself while he studied, Hillel worked as a water carrier. Everyday after work, he took some of his money and bought enough food for just one meal.

With the rest of the money he paid to enter the House of Study so he could listen to the words of the Rabbis.

One Friday morning Hillel could not find any work. He had no money to buy wine or bread for his Sabbath meals. He didn't even have enough money for a small snack to keep his stomach from rumbling.

But what troubled him most of all was that he couldn't pay to enter the House of Study.

"Maybe I can still hear the words of my teachers if I stand outside the House of Study," he thought. So Hillel went and stood beside the building. He put his ear to the wall, but he couldn't hear a thing.

Then Hillel remembered that there was a big window – a skylight – up on the roof.

"I wonder if I'd be able to hear from up there?" he thought, looking up to the top of the building.

It was difficult climbing up to the top, and even a little scary, but finally Hillel reached the skylight.

He lay down on the big window, pressed his ear against the glass, and listened to the words of the Rabbis.

Even though it was winter, Hillel stayed up there all day long. He was so excited about being able to learn from the Rabbis, he didn't feel the bitter cold. He didn't even realize that it had begun to snow!

Evening came. The Rabbis and students in the House of Study welcomed the Sabbath together, sang the

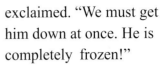

evening prayers and went home to their families for the Sabbath meal.

But where was Hillel? Hillel had fainted from the cold. He lay on the roof, under the falling snow, all night long.

In the morning, the sun came out. The Rabbis returned to the House of Study for morning prayers.

Shemaya turned to Avtalyon and asked, "If the sun is so strong today, why is it still dark in the study hall?"

"Look!" cried Avtalyon as he glanced up at the big window, pointing at the shadow above them. "There is a man lying on the skylight!"

The students rushed up to the roof as quickly as they could. When they reached the man, they were astonished.

"This is our friend, Hillel!" they exclaimed. "We must get him down at once. He is completely frozen!"

When Shemaya saw Hillel's frozen body, he prayed with all his might.

"May God help this dear, devoted student recover completely. Surely he will one day be a great scholar, for who has ever seen such love of learning as this!"

Avtalyon ordered the students to light a fire in order to warm up Hillel's frozen body. "Even though it is the Sabbath," he told them, "and we are not permitted to light a fire, we may disregard the laws of Sabbath in order to save a life."

Hillel recovered and continued to learn every day in the House of Study. He studied for many years until he became a great scholar, a devoted teacher, and a deeply respected leader of the People of Israel.

NOW CONSIDER THIS:

✳ *Why did Hillel leave his family and go to Israel?*

✳ *Do you think someone should have helped Hillel pay for his studies?*

✳ *Why do you think it is permitted to disobey the laws of Sabbath in order to save a life?*

✳ *What other laws of Sabbath do you know?*

Yosef's Love Of The Sabbath

Babylonian Talmud. Shabbat 119A

Once there was a poor Jewish family who lived in a simple hut at the edge of a village. Yosef, the father, worked long hours chopping firewood in the forest and hauling it to the nearby town to sell. All week long, Yosef and his family dressed in old clothes. They ate just bread and potatoes. But on the seventh day, the Sabbath, they put on their finest clothes, prayed and sang, studied the Torah and ate only the best foods.

One Sabbath evening, while Yosef and his family were sitting around the table, there was a loud knock at the door. The local landlord appeared.

"Yosef," the landlord shouted. "I need a load of firewood right away!"

Yosef's children trembled with fear. But Yosef wasn't afraid. He answered the landlord politely, "I'm sorry, sir, but as you know, I don't work on the Sabbath."

The landlord was furious. "Go out and chop the wood for me immediately," he hissed, "or I will drive you and your family out of this village!"

Yosef was unshaken. "I'm sorry, sir. I can't help you," he said again, calmly.

Now the landlord was fuming. "Suit yourself! I'll find someone else to bring me wood, and you will leave the village!"

With that, the landlord left, slamming the door behind him.

That night the landlord had a scary dream. In his dream, he was visited by a messenger from the king. "Landlord," the messenger said, "the king has decreed that Yosef, who loves and honors the Sabbath, will soon get all your worldly possessions."

The landlord woke up, trembling. "What should I do?" he wondered. Then he had an idea.

The next morning, the landlord sold his house and everything he owned. With the money, he bought a large, beautiful diamond. Of course, he had to

44

hide the diamond from robbers, so he sewed it into his hat and put the hat snugly on his head."Now Yosef will never get my money," he thought, smiling. Then the landlord headed out of the village to get far away from Yosef.

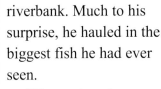

As he was crossing a bridge, a gust of wind suddenly blew the hat, with the diamond, into the river. The landlord almost jumped in after it, but the water was deep and icy cold, and besides, he couldn't swim.

"My diamond!" the landlord cried. But no one heard him. The landlord sat down on the bridge and wept. Then he travelled to a distant land.

For many months the hat lay at the bottom of the river. Finally, it began to rot. The diamond fell free from the threads that held it in place. One day a large fish swam by. Thinking that the sparkling diamond would make a tasty meal, the fish swallowed it and happily swam along.

That afternoon one of the village fishermen cast his line from the riverbank. Much to his surprise, he hauled in the biggest fish he had ever seen.

"I know just the person who will want this fish," the fisherman thought.

The fisherman hurried to Yosef's hut. "Would you like to buy this splendid fish?" he asked.

"Of course," said Yosef. "This will be a fine way to honor the Sabbath."

Yosef handed over the money he'd saved up all week long and bought the fish. The whole family watched as Yosef placed the huge fish on the table. He cut it open and there, inside its belly, was a magnificent diamond!

"Look what a treasure God has sent us!" Yosef's daughter exclaimed. "Now our parents won't have to work so hard."

And so Yosef and his family were rewarded for their love of the Sabbath. From then on they lived in comfort. And they were always able to share their joyful Sabbath with many guests.

NOW CONSIDER THIS:

✳ *What would you have said to the landlord if you were in Yosef's place?*

✳ *Do you think the family was able to forget their worries and continue their joyful meal? Could you do that?*

✳ *Why did the fisherman think of taking the big fish to Yosef?*